CAMPING GUIDE

WILD JOBS

LAURA K. MURRAY

CREATIVE EDUCATION · CREATIVE PAPERBACKS

PUBLISHED BY CREATIVE EDUCATION AND CREATIVE PAPERBACKS
P.O. Box 227, Mankato, Minnesota 56002
Creative Education and Creative Paperbacks are
imprints of The Creative Company
www.thecreativecompany.us

DESIGN AND PRODUCTION by Joe Kahnke
Art direction by Rita Marshall
Printed in the United States of America

PHOTOGRAPHS by Alamy (13UG 13th, Ian Dagnall, Horizon International
Images Limited, D. Hurst, imageBROKER, LOOK Die Bildagentur der
Fotografen GmbH, Namibia, Whit Richardson), Getty Images (Blend
Images – Michael DeYoung, James + Courtney Forte, WIN-Initiative),
LostandTaken.com, Shutterstock (Galyna Andrushko, Alex Brylov,
Butterfly Hunter, Gambarini Gianandrea, Mat Hayward, anthony heflin,
Husjak, Betti Luna, Nik Merkulov, Miloje, BOONCHUAY PROMJIAM,
Sergiy Zavgorodny)

Library of Congress Cataloging-in-Publication Data
Names: Murray, Laura K., author.
Title: Camping guide / Laura K. Murray.
Series: Wild Jobs.
Includes bibliographical references and index.
Summary: A brief exploration of what camping guides do on the job,
including the equipment they use and the training they need, plus real-
life instances of camping guides working in America's state and national
parks.
Identifiers: ISBN 978-1-60818-922-9 (hardcover) / ISBN 978-1-62832-
538-6 (pbk) / ISBN 978-1-56660-974-6 (eBook)
This title has been submitted for CIP processing under LCCN 2017940119.

CCSS: RI.1.1, 2, 3, 4, 5, 6, 7; RI.2.1, 2, 4, 5, 6; RI.3.1, 2, 5, 7; RF.1.1, 3, 4; RF.2.3, 4

FIRST EDITION HC 9 8 7 6 5 4 3 2 1
FIRST EDITION PBK 9 8 7 6 5 4 3 2 1

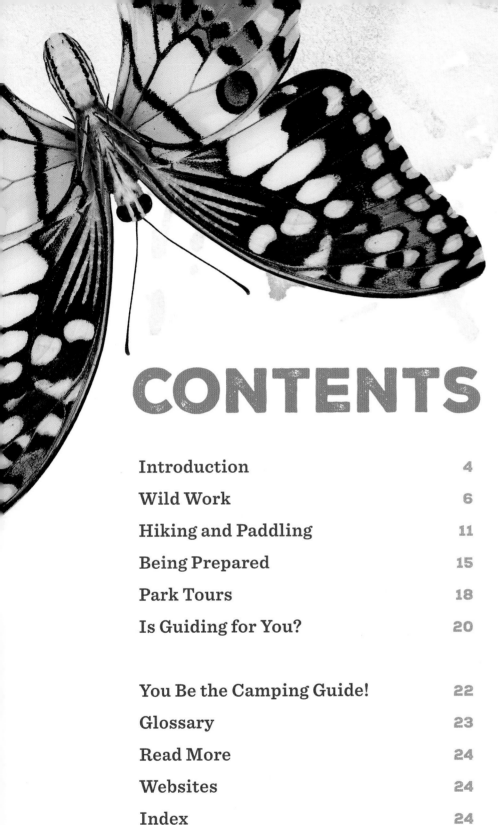

CONTENTS

THE NIGHT AIR IS CRISP.

But you stay warm inside your soft sleeping bag. Wind rustles the trees. In the distance, a wolf howls. A lone moose bellows.

1
WILD WORK

Camping guides lead people through the wilderness. They share information about the area's **FLORA** and **FAUNA**. They keep their camping groups safe.

Camping guides prepare the camping gear. They plan each day's activities. They cook meals on the trail. They enjoy the wild, beautiful outdoors.

HIKING AND PADDLING

Camping guides may work in the mountains, forests, or deserts. They hike for miles over all kinds of **TERRAIN**. It might be muddy and wet or hot and dry. It might be cold and snowy. Some groups even hike on **GLACIERS**.

Sometimes camping guides take people out on the water. They paddle kayaks, canoes, or paddleboards. They ride in rafts. The water churns fast. Its spray is cold!

PADDLEBOARDS

BEING PREPARED

Camping guides learn about the land's history, rocks, plants, and animals. Many camping guides take first-aid courses. They may earn a **CERTIFICATION** in wilderness leadership.

MAP

Camping guides do not want people to get hurt or lost. They bring food, water, and flashlights. They have tents and sleeping bags. They bring matches and a first-aid kit. They have a map or **COMPASS**. They carry bear spray for protection.

PARK TOURS

Many camping guides lead groups through state and national parks. The most-visited national park in the United States is Great Smoky Mountains. More than 10 million people go there each year.

5
IS GUIDING FOR YOU?

Camping guides like meeting new people and spending time outdoors. Would *you* want to be a camping guide when you grow up?

YOU BE THE CAMPING GUIDE!

Imagine you are a camping guide. Read the questions below about your wild job. Then write your answers on a separate sheet of paper. Draw a picture of yourself as a camping guide!

My name is _____. I am a camping guide.

1. What sounds do you hear in the woods?
2. What foods do you cook while camping?
3. What types of gear do you bring?
4. What is your favorite part of being a camping guide?
5. Where do you want to explore next?

GLOSSARY

CERTIFICATION: proof of certain skills

COMPASS: an object used to show direction

FAUNA: animals of a region or habitat

FLORA: plants of a region or habitat

GLACIERS: large bodies of ice that move very slowly

TERRAIN: the physical features of an area of land

READ MORE

Champion, Neil. *Wild Trail: Hiking and Camping.* Mankato, Minn.: Smart Apple Media, 2013.

Morey, Allan. *Camping.* North Mankato, Minn.: Amicus, 2017.

WEBSITES

History of the National Parks
http://kids.nationalgeographic.com/explore/history/history-of-the-national-parks/#park-yellowstone.jpg
Learn fun facts about U.S. national parks.

Solo Sports: Walking and Hiking
http://pbskids.org/itsmylife/body/solosports/article6.html
Read about hiking, walking, and other activities.

Note: Every effort has been made to ensure that the websites listed above are suitable for children, that they have educational value, and that they contain no inappropriate material. However, because of the nature of the Internet, it is impossible to guarantee that these sites will remain active indefinitely or that their contents will not be altered.

INDEX